I am Mallorie

Selective mutism awareness by:

Patricia L. McIntosh
Andrea Johnson ARNP, PMHNP-BC
Sara K. McIntosh

Illustrations by photographer Juls Yungtum

I praise you because I am fearfully and wonderfully made. Psalms 139:14

To order additional copies of this book, contact:
Xlibris
844-714-8691
www.Xlibris.com
Orders@Xlibris.com

References:
DSM-5 (2013) - Diagnostic and Statistical
Manual of Mental Disorders
Scripture quotations are taken from the Holy Bible

ISBN: Softcover   978-1-6641-6562-5
        Hardcover   978-1-6641-6644-8
        EBook   978-1-6641-6561-8

Print information available on the last page

Rev. date: 04/13/2021

Introduction by Grandma Pat

<u>I am Mallorie</u> tells the story of my granddaughter who was diagnosed with selective mutism, an anxiety disorder that causes her to be silent in some social situations or unfamiliar surroundings. The Bible tells us that we are fearfully and wonderfully made. That doesn't mean we are designed to be fearful. According to the Hebrew translation, fearfully means heartfelt and wonderfully means unique. I'm an artist. When I create something, I put my heart into my work trying to make sure it is my own unique design. That's how God has created each of us. Mallorie is no exception. She's exactly as God intended for her to be. I wish anxiety didn't cause her to hold back her voice and the world could see the witty, free-spirited little girl that her family and I see, but that's not for me to decide. We will just continue to encourage, love, and support her as the beautiful gift she is.

Before I started writing, <u>I Am Mallorie</u>, I needed permission from three very important people. First off, Mallorie herself. I didn't want to write something that would add to her anxiety and I didn't want to slow the progress she has made to communicate in public. I also needed approval from her mom and dad. As Mallorie's Grandma I don't have the first right to tell her story. It's my son Lyle and his wife Sara's job to raise her and to decide how, when, and if her story would be told. With that being said I'd like to thank them for not only giving the book their blessing, but for Sara contributing to it with a parent letter.

I'd also like to thank Andrea Johnson for her message. You may have noticed that her name is followed by a long list of official letters, but to Mallorie she's just Aunt Andrea. Her education in mental illness and having spent a considerable amount of time with Mallorie, provides Aunt Andrea a unique view point and I'm pleased she is willing to share her thoughts with us on selective mutism.

The story book photos included in this book were created by our friend Juls Yungtum. My grandkids had a couple opportunities to work with Juls on greenscreen photography projects. Mallorie is comfortable with her so it only seemed right to ask her to design the story book pages. Mallorie is hoping that kids will love the images as much as she enjoyed modeling for them. Thank you, Juls, for providing the creative illustrations.

I pray this book is a blessing to the readers. If you picked it up because you know a child that is socially silent, remember all children are a unique gift from God and they are fearfully and wonderfully made.

Patricia L McIntosh

I am Mallorie

By: Patricia L. McIntosh

In honor of Mallorie, let your light shine, sweet girl.
Dedicated to children with social anxiety.

I am Mallorie.
I am fearfully and
wonderfully made.

When I am with my family,
I play, I dance, I sing,
and I shout out loud.
I like to talk,
A LOT.

When I'm home,
I feel happy
and brave.

When I'm with
some people
I'm silent
because I have
selective mutism.

When I'm not at home, I don't speak. I feel uneasy and my body is uncomfortable. When I have those feelings, my voice hides.

I'm not just shy, I'm
not being stubborn,
I'm not trying to be rude.
Anxiety can cause me to
hold back my words.

I can communicate with you if you ask me yes and no questions, or I can write you a message.

It might look like I
have a secret because
sometimes I share my
words with a whisper.

Even if I'm not ready to speak to you, we can be friends. I'm outgoing and I like to have fun.

My buddies and I like to be silly and play together. When I feel comfortable, I will talk, but it could take awhile, so be patient.

If you hear my voice, please don't act surprised. It might cause me to be quiet again.

I am fearfully and wonderfully made. I am happy and brave. I am Mallorie.

A message from Aunt Andrea

According to the Diagnostic and Statistical Manual of Mental Disorders (DSM-5, 2013), Selective Mutism is when someone fails to speak during social interactions where you would normally expect them to. With children it is typically at school or in public when their anxiety gets high and they are unable to find their voice. Even though I studied the disorder and have personal experience with a diagnosed child I wouldn't consider myself an expert on selective mutism simply because each child presents differently. It takes an individualized approach for every patient to figure out what strategies help them to be successful.

I feel fortunate that I happen to be one of the people Mallorie feels comfortable communicating with. I like to think she enjoys talking with me because I try to make her laugh. For example, occasionally she joins my family at a restaurant, we go over the menu so she can plan what to order beforehand, this helps her feel like she's in control. When it's time to order, I try to keep the moment light. I might tell her, "Ask for whatever you want even if it's purple unicorns- the worst that can happen is they will tell you they don't have purple unicorns." This usually makes her giggle and might help her relax and order her food. She can always fall back on whispering to me to order for her too.

Another way to gauge your child's reactions is to ask yourself, "Would I be, or am I anxious in this situation?" If the answer is yes, it is logical that a child would pick up on that anxiety and also become anxious. The best practice for helping children with social anxiety is to create a safe environment. Try not to force change. For Mallorie, as people made comments like, "I'm going to get you to talk to me," she became more and more fearful around talking. Fear about people hearing her voice and what their reactions would be. Basically, this disorder requires a lot of education to all the care providers, educators, and peers of the child to help ease their anxiety. Some patience and grace are needed to help each child work through their concerns in social situations to find better coping mechanisms and allow them to find ways to communicate.

One thing that has helped Mallorie is that even though sometimes she is not comfortable talking, her parents did a good job of continually exposing her to many situations. These are not kids that you want to hide away. Continually exposing Mallorie to crowds, school, and events allowed her to gradually figure out how to communicate both verbally and non-verbally and reduce her anxiousness. While this may still be an issue she continues to work through, she is gradually finding ways to quickly cope in all settings. I am encouraged with each breakthrough Mallorie has and watching her blossom has been heartwarming.

Andrea Johnson ARNP, PMHNP-BC

A message from Mommy

"Oh, Mallorie, she's the shy one, right?" This phrase is common to hear as Mallorie's mother. It's a frustrating comment, but at the same time it shows that information about this silent anxiety needs to be shared. Mallorie is a sweet, spunky 7-year-old who loves to sing, dance, and tell jokes. She has been coping with this social disorder since she was 3 years old.

Mallorie first halted verbal communication at daycare after her provider moved into a brand-new, unfamiliar house, and she began attending preschool. She was not vocal with her peers or teachers, and even ceased communicating with some extended family members. It was so difficult to wrap our minds around what was going on because she was so confident and chatty with us at home. We would even go in public and she would communicate with strangers. For example, she would say "please," and "thank you" to the bank teller for giving her a sucker. We knew this wasn't just a child being shy since she seemed to be more comfortable with strangers than people she was around regularly. After getting some assistance from our school speech and language pathologist along with our family physician, we learned Mallorie was dealing with the social anxiety called selective mutism. We observed her more closely and noticed that her chest would tighten up in certain situations. She would say to us, "I really want to speak, but the words just won't come out." It's definitely heartbreaking witnessing your young child go through this especially when there isn't one single thing you can do to make it go away.

As Mallorie has grown we have found ways to help her cope with her anxiety symptoms. We continue to encourage her to participate in every social opportunity offered. She's tried out for our small town "Little Miss" competitions, enjoys being active in 4H, and enthusiastically joins her friends in community athletic little league teams. Communicating the dos and don'ts of selective mutism has been key to share with all of those who get the privilege of being a part of Mallorie's journey. At school, the speech and language pathologist help Mallorie set weekly goals when it comes to different forms of communication. It is not rare to observe her nonverbally communicating with her friends such as flashing a smile, using hand motions, writing a message, and using facial expressions. She has also become more comfortable making sounds. She isn't afraid to share an out loud laugh with her buddies! It's been a slow process, but with each small step she makes the layers of anxiety that mask her vibrant personality slowly begin to peel back.

Mallorie is very excited to be an advocate for herself and others who experience social anxiety by sharing her story with you. Our hope is to provide awareness, and promote early intervention. Every child deserves to be understood and thrive, even if they are silent.

Sara K. McIntosh

Printed in the United States
by Baker & Taylor Publisher Services